The Little Child in the Sky

written and illustrated by
Alexandra Stoll

Excalibur Publishing
New York

For Diana, Kai, and Vivie

Published by:
Excalibur Publishing
434 Avenue of the Americas, Suite 790
New York, New York 10011

Book Design and Art Direction: Kara Glasgold, Griffin Design

Library of Congress Cataloging-in-Publication Data

Stoll, Alexandra, date.
  The little child in the sky / written and illustrated by Alexandra
Stoll.
       p. cm.
  Summary: A little child waits in the sky, where there is no fear,
until a light lets the child know it is time to be born on Earth.
  ISBN 0-9627226-7-7 (paperback)
  [1. Childbirth--Fiction.]   I. Title.
PZ7.S875834L1 1993   93-20692
[E]--dc20   CIP
                                            AC

Printed in the United States of America

10 9 8 7 6 5 4 3 2 1

Once upon a time...

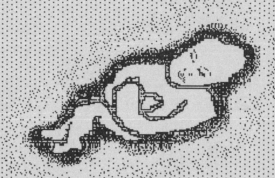

...there was a little child
    waiting to be born.

Everyone loved the child dearly, but no one knew yet who it was to be.

How sad!

The poor child waited and waited.

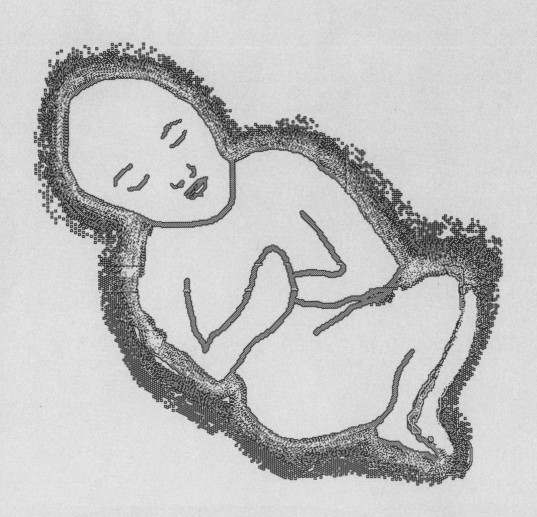

Sometimes the child thought it was possible to see the right parents down on Earth.
"I know that's my mother! I just know it is! She's Chinese! Just like I dreamed she would be! She's beautiful!"

But it wasn't the mother. It was just a woman in China, washing her clothes, dreaming of what it would be like to have a little child.

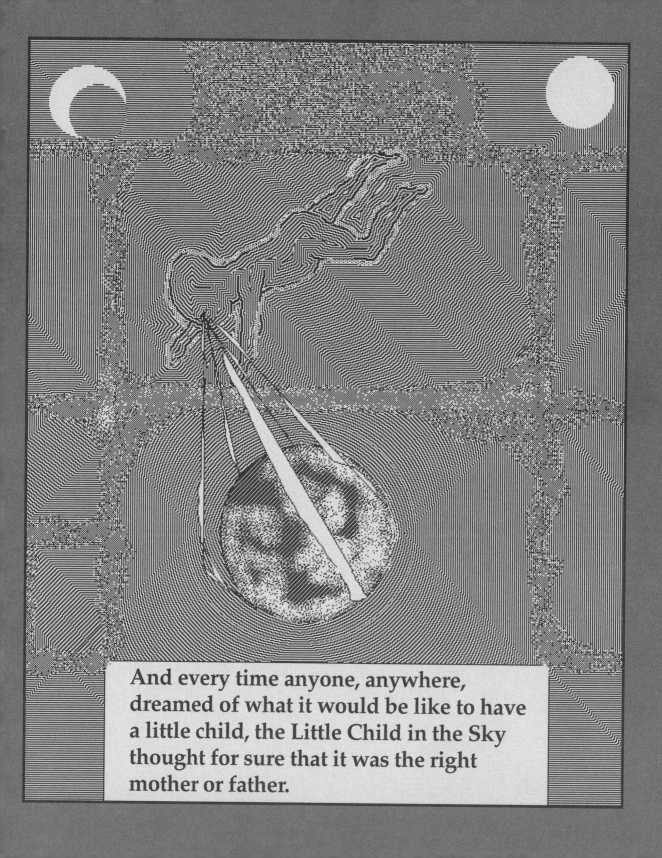

And every time anyone, anywhere, dreamed of what it would be like to have a little child, the Little Child in the Sky thought for sure that it was the right mother or father.

Because that is how little girls and boys start on Earth, sometimes, from somebody wondering what it would be like to have a child.

After a very, very long time, the little child thought that perhaps everyone had forgotten, that there would never be a mother or father, and coming to Earth would never happen.

The child had been

    watching

      and

        waiting,

          hoping every minute

            that it was time to be next.

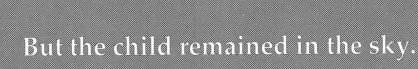
But the child remained in the sky.

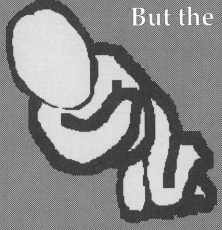

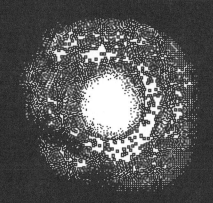

One lovely day,

a bright light appeared

quite far away.

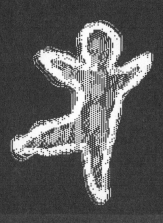

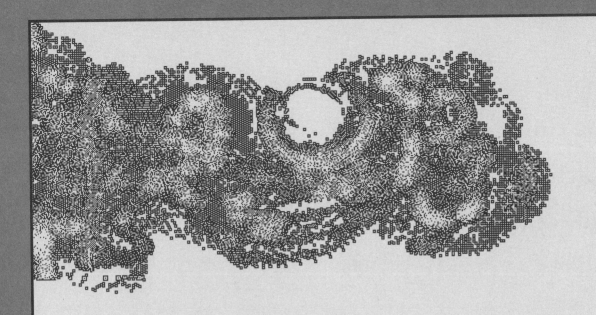

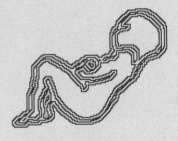

At first, it was covered
by a cloud, and the
little child could
barely see it
in the distance.

The child
watched
and watched...

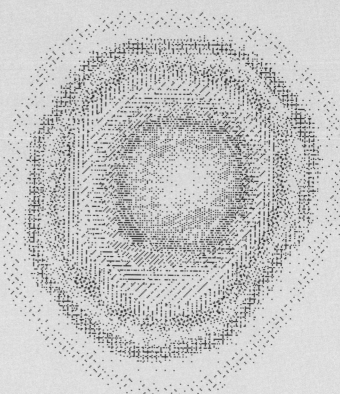

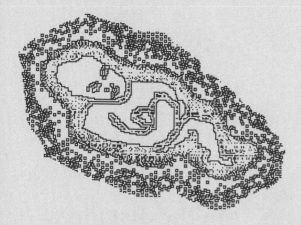

...as the light
got brighter
and
brighter.

It melted the cloud away and came rushing toward the child.

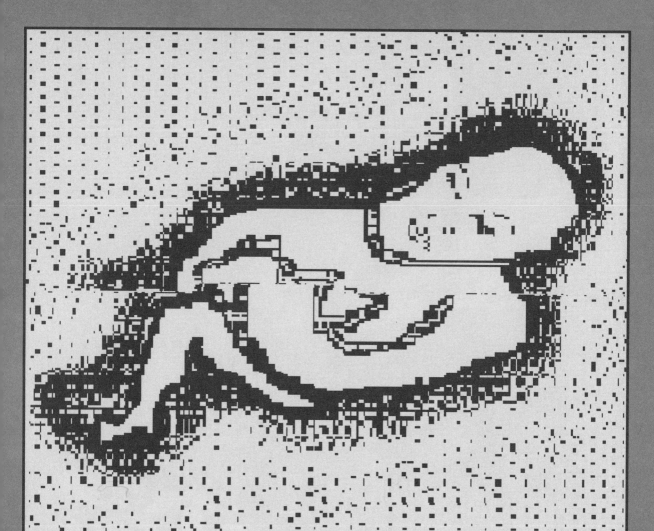

The little
child
was not
scared.

In the sky
there is no
such thing
as fear.

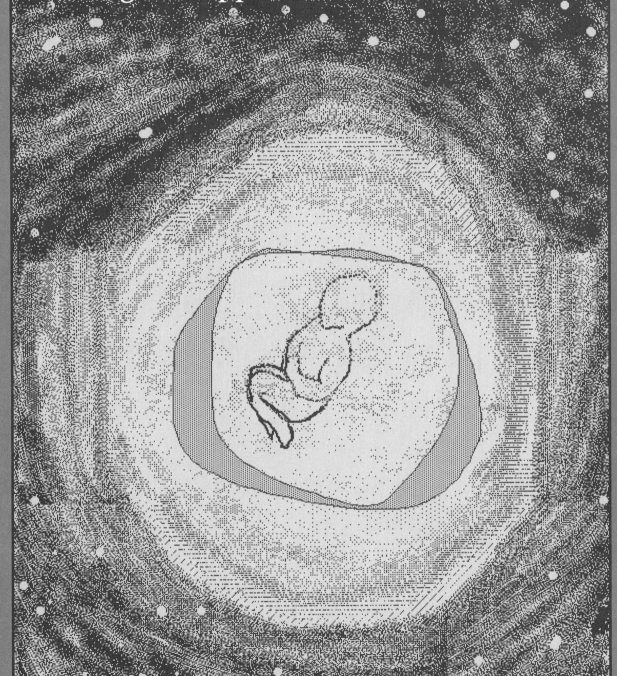

The light wrapped itself around the child.

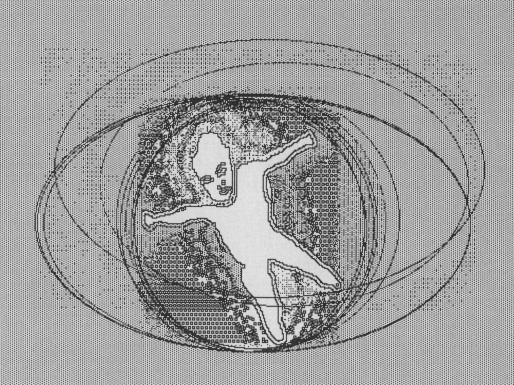

It was warm and soft.

It seemed to go
right through the child.

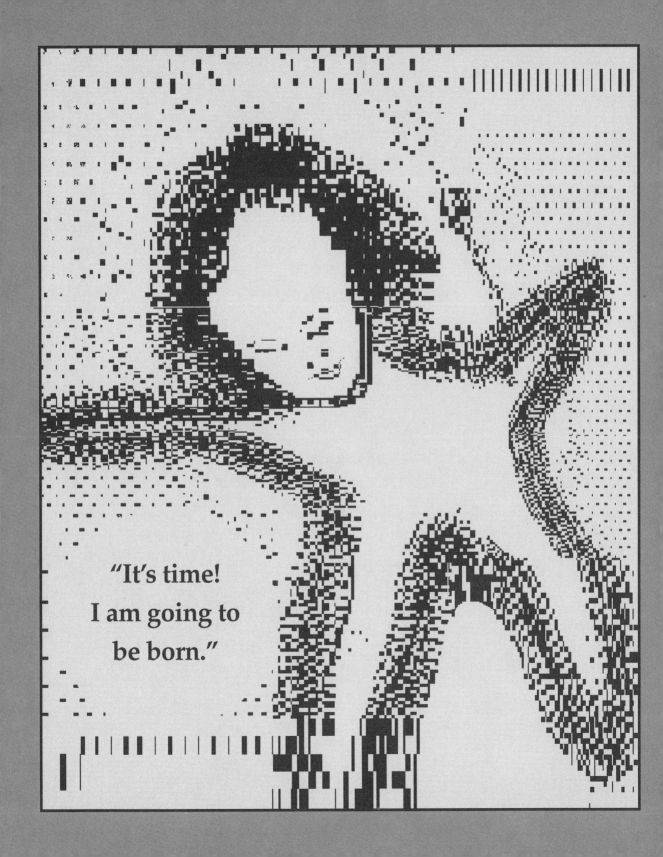

As
the
light held
the child
tightly in its
warmth, it said,
with no words,
"It's your time.
It's your time."

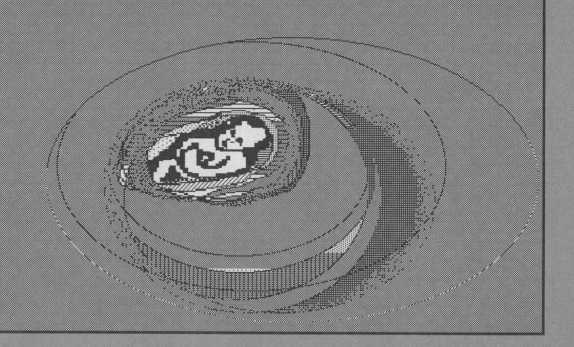

The little child smiled,
with no mouth,
and laughed with delight.

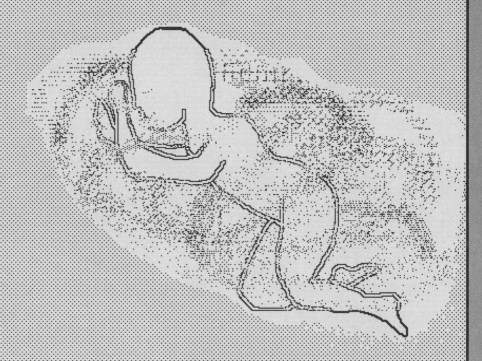

The little child
laughed again.

"But that is what
I do now!"

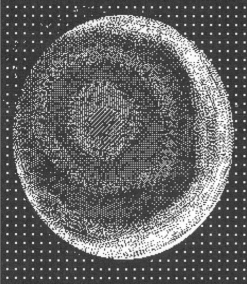

"Yes, but,

On Earth, things are quite different..."

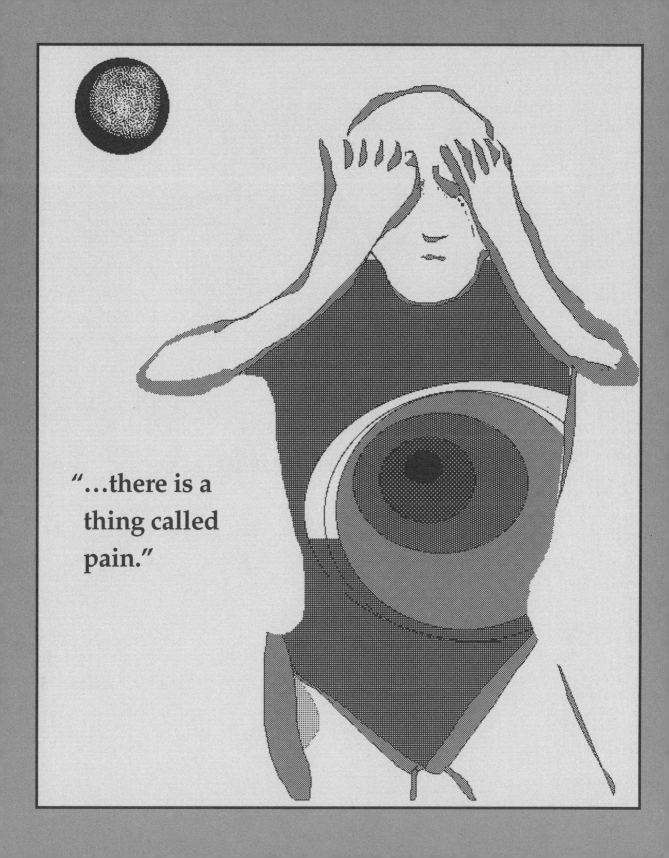

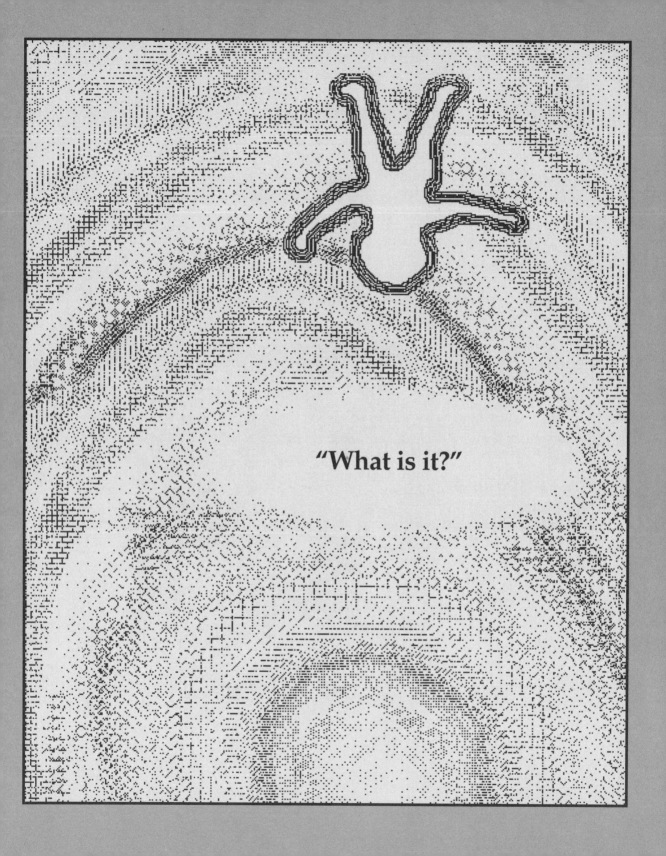

"What is it?"

"You can only know pain by being alive," said the light.

The light needed
no answer, for it
knew what the
little child wanted.

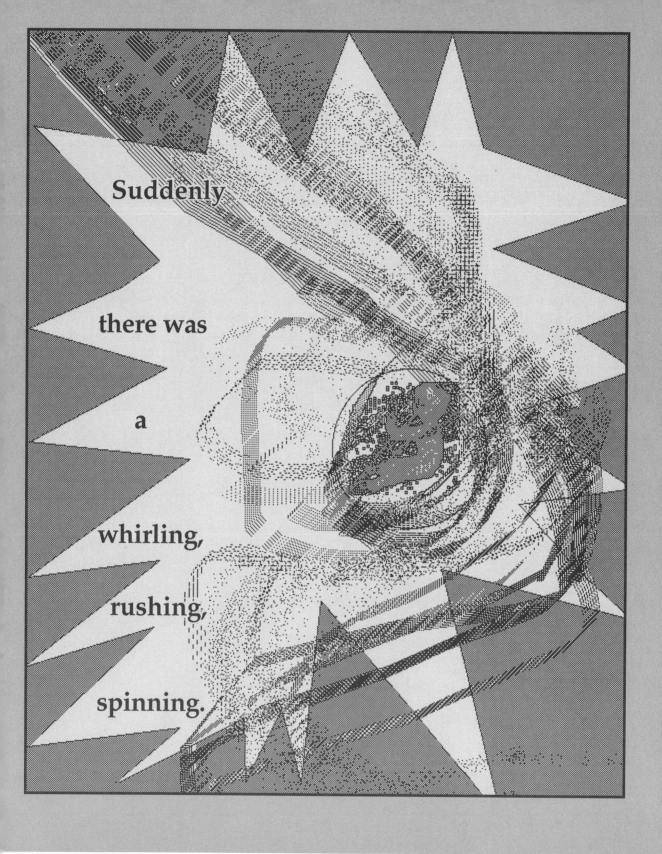

Suddenly

there was

a

whirling,

rushing,

spinning.

Something closed tightly around the little child, and the light was gone. In the darkness, there were only speckles of light floating softly.

A beating.   A pump.

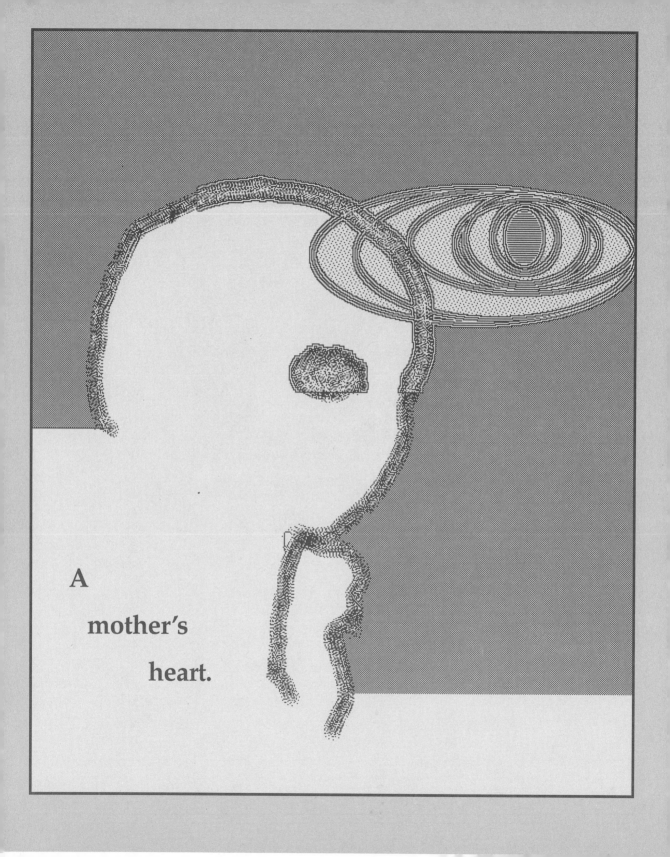

A

mother's

heart.

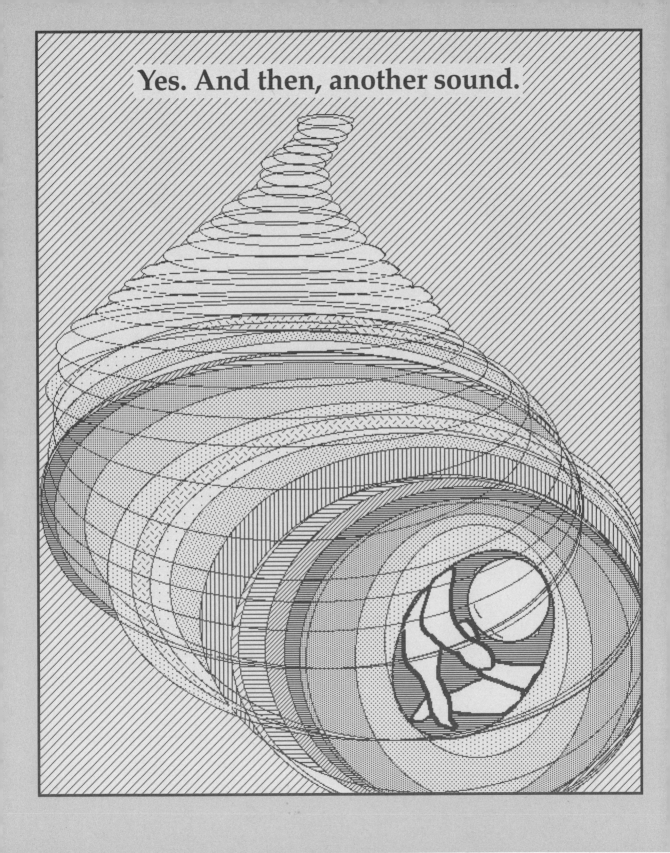

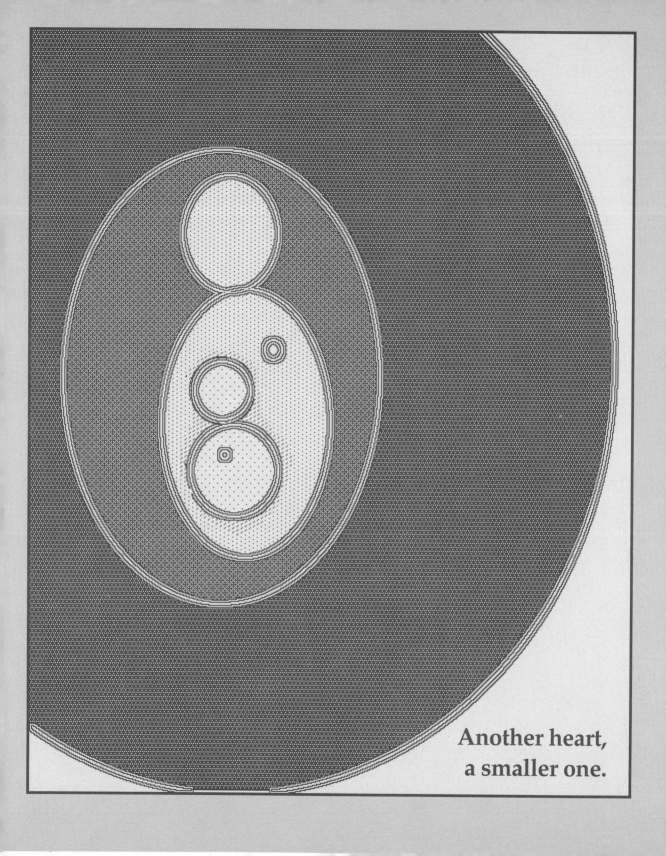

Another heart,
a smaller one.

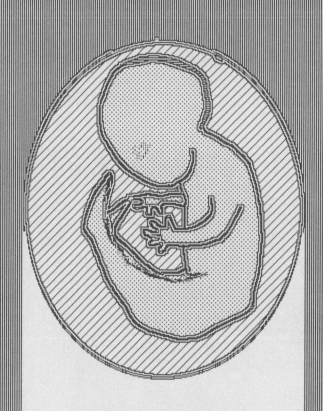

Two little feet...

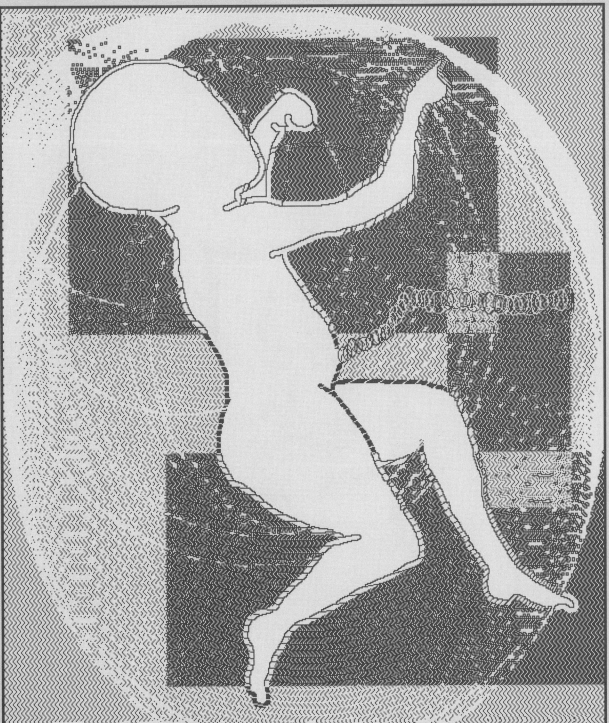

The child began moving…touching…

Am

I

all

alone?

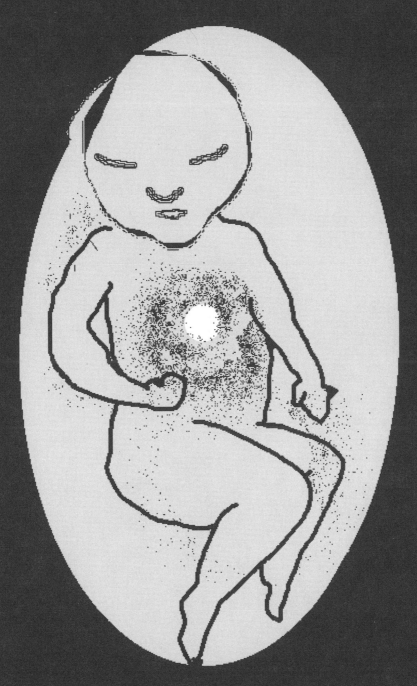

"I'm here...in here," said the light.

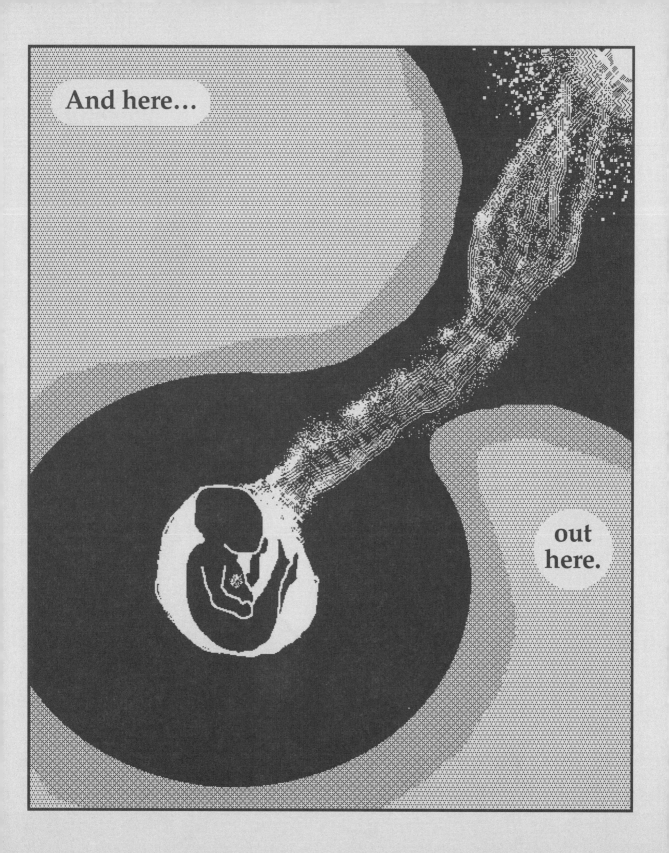

And so, the little child came into the world.

And in the world, there was pain...

And there was JOY!